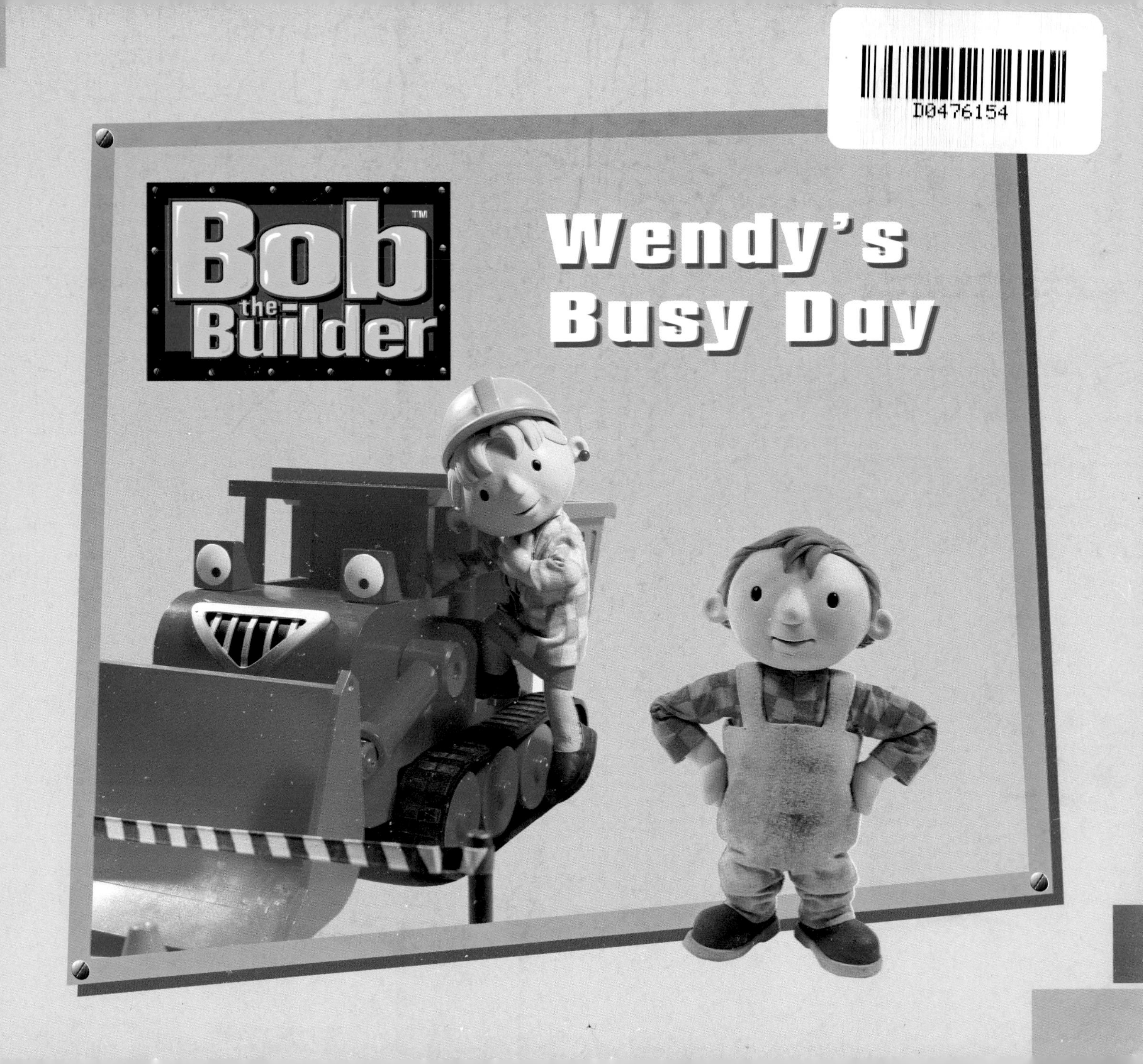
Bob the Builder™
Wendy's Busy Day

One cold Monday morning, Wendy walked into Bob's front room and found him in his chair by the fire, wrapped in a blanket.

"**A-a-a-a-choo!**" sneezed Bob.

"Goodness, you look ill!" cried Wendy.

"I am ill!" sniffed Bob. "I've dot a really bad dold!"

"You'd better stay indoors and keep warm," said Wendy.

"I can't do that!" spluttered Bob. "We've dot a big resurfacing job to do on the main road into town – it's dot to be finished by five o'clock tonight."

"I know," said Wendy. "Why don't *I* go out with the machines? After all, either the work gets done with me supervising – or it doesn't get done at all."

"**A-a-a-tchoo!**" sneezed Bob.

"I'll tell the machines," said Wendy as she headed briskly out of the door.

Pilchard pushed her food dish forwards.

"Miaow!" she mewed.

"I dow you want your breakfast," Bob told her, "but I..."

Bob stopped as another huge sneeze tickled his nose.

"**A-a-a-a-tchoo!**" he sneezed.

"Miaow!" yowled Pilchard, hungrily.

"Bob's got a *very* bad cold," Wendy told the machines. "He's going to stay indoors until he gets better."

"How will we do the resurfacing without Bob?" fretted Scoop.

"You've got *me*!" smiled Wendy.

"Hurray!" cheered the machines.

"Right, I'll stay behind to look after Bob," said Scoop.

"I think I will, too," said Lofty, shyly.

Wendy hopped on board Muck.

"Can we fix it?" she called.

"**Yes, we can!**" yelled the team.

And they roared out of the yard.

Wendy gulped with surprise when she saw the big potholes in the road.

"Oh, dear, it's *very* bumpy," she said.

Roley chuckled. "Hey, Wendy, flattening bumps is *my* job!" he said.

"Okay!" smiled Wendy. "Let's do it!"

Back at home, Bob sat sneezing. "Doh..." he muttered, as he wiped his nose.

"Are you feeling better?" called Scoop, from outside the window.

"I feel *dewwible*!" wheezed Bob.

On the town road, Dizzy mixed concrete so that the team could fill in a big pothole.

Then Muck roared up. "Here it comes," he yelled, as he lifted his dumper to tip out the sticky road surface.

"I'm right behind you!" rumbled Roley, as he moved in to flatten everything out.

S-Q-U-E-L-C-H!

Wendy beamed and clapped.

"That looks *perfect!*" she cried.

As Dizzy moved over to give Roley more room, she spotted an old football lying by the side of the road.

"Oooh! Look what I've found!" she squeaked excitedly, as she tapped it with her front wheel.

"And Dizzy's got the ball," she cried, as she chased after it. "She's racing down the wing. Is she going to score...?"

"No! Stop!" yelled Wendy, as Dizzy headed for the sticky, wet road surface.

Dizzy didn't hear.

"She's scored!" shouted the little cement mixer – and landed **splat** in the sticky stuff.

"Awww!" wailed Dizzy, as she watched her wheels slowly sinking. "I'm stuck!"

"Don't worry!" gasped Wendy. "We'll get you out!"

"How?" rumbled Roley. "If we go in there we'll get stuck as well!"

"You've got to do *something*," shrieked Dizzy. "You can't just leave me here to set like a rock!"

"I'll phone Bob," said Wendy.

"Yes, phone Bob. He'll know what to do," said Muck.

Wendy started to dial Bob's number. Then she stopped.

"No," she said firmly. "Bob's ill. We must fix this ourselves."

The machines stared hopefully at Wendy.

"We can't go *in*," she reasoned. "But Dizzy has to be pulled *out*. How do we do that...?"

"I've got it!" roared Muck. "It's Lofty we need. He'll pull Dizzy out in a flash!"

"Good thinking, Muck!" cried Wendy.

"We've got to be quick though," added Muck. "Jump on, Wendy."

Muck whizzed back to the yard.

"Lofty! Scoop!" Muck yelled as he screeched to a stop.

"You two are back early..." said Lofty, in surprise.

"Lofty – we need your help!" cried Wendy.

"Dizzy's stuck in some concrete and we need you to pull her out quickly!" chugged Muck.

"Lofty to the rescue!" smiled Lofty.

Bob was snoozing in his armchair when he was woken by the machines revving out of the yard.

"Scoop!" Bob called, opening the front door. "What was all dat doise dat woke me up? And where's Lofty gone?"

Scoop wriggled uncomfortably.

"Oh, er... he went to see how the others were getting on," he replied.

"Well, it's four o'clock dow," fretted Bob. "So they've only got an hour before the road reopens. Doh, dear..." he sighed to Pilchard. "I hope everything is going smoothly..."

Things weren't going at *all* smoothly on the town road. Lofty lowered his big metal hook towards Dizzy's handle.

"Get a grip, Dizzy!" he clanked.

"Got it!" squeaked Dizzy, as the hook locked on. "**Pull!**"

Lofty nervously pulled Dizzy up – but suddenly he lost his grip. Dizzy crashed to the ground.

"Try again!" yelled Dizzy, crossly.

Holding their breath, Wendy, Roley and Muck watched Lofty's winching machinery strain under the pressure.

Slowly, very slowly, Lofty hauled Dizzy free of the concrete.

"Yes!" squealed Dizzy, as he gently lowered her down onto the ground.

"Hooray for Lofty!" cheered Wendy.

"Thank you... thank you..." giggled Dizzy in relief.

"Oh, goodness," gasped Wendy, as she looked at her watch. "Look at the time – we've only got half an hour left. Come on – let's finish the road!"

Tick-tock ticked the clock, as the machines worked as hard as they could.

With Wendy supervising, Muck tipped the last load of road surface for Roley to flatten.

DONG! DONG! DONG! DONG! DONG!

"Five o'clock!" yelled Wendy. "Time to open the road!"

Quickly, Lofty cleared away the safety barriers. Everyone gathered around the tape blocking off the road.

In a loud voice, Wendy said, "I now pronounce the town road open!"

And she snipped through the tape with a pair of scissors.

"Hooray!" cheered the machines.

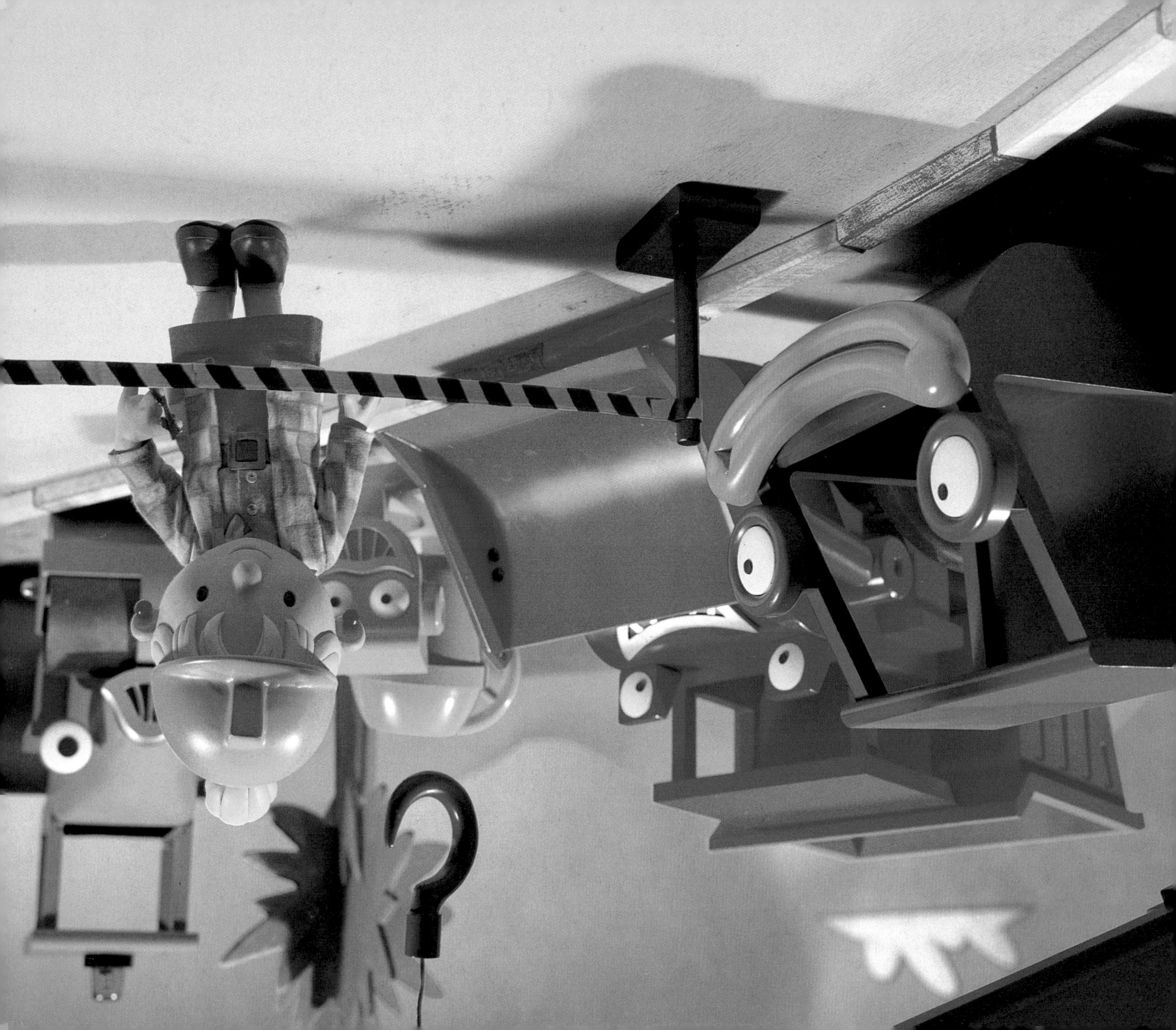

The first vehicle to use the resurfaced road was Travis, with Spud on the back.

"What's going on here?" called Travis.

"We've just done a job – without Bob," squeaked Dizzy.

"We've mended the road with Wendy!" roared Muck.

Spud inspected the newly resurfaced road.

"You've missed a bit," he said, pointing at the ground.

"Where?" asked Dizzy, as the team looked down at the road.

"It looks perfect to me," said Wendy, anxiously.

"Only teasing," laughed Spud. "It looks perfect to me too! Hah hah hah!"

Back at the yard, Bob hurried out to meet everybody.

"We did it, Bob!" called Wendy. "We finished the road!"

"Wad a deam!" croaked Bob. "Dank you all so much."

"Um... it's cold out here," fretted Lofty. "Shouldn't you get back indoors, Bob?"

"Better do as you're told," teased Wendy.

"Okay... okay," laughed Bob. "I'll have an early night."

Wendy yawned an enormous yawn.

"We *all* need an early night," she said.

Later that night, just as the machines were drifting off to sleep, Dizzy nudged Muck's undercarriage.

"Muck," she whispered.

"Um...?" mumbled Muck.

"Wasn't that a great goal I scored today?" said Dizzy.

Muck opened his mouth to reply but something started tickling the back of his nose.

"**A-a-a-a-a-at-chhoo!**" he sneezed.

"Now Muck's got Bob's cold!" chuckled Scoop.

**"A-a-a-a-
t-choo!"**

sneezed Muck.

THE END!